MONSTER HUNTERS
tame tahoe tessie

by Jan Fields
Illustrated by Scott Brundage

Calico

An Imprint of Magic Wagon
www.abdopublishing.com

www.abdopublishing.com

Published by Magic Wagon, a division of ABDO, PO Box 398166, Minneapolis, Minnesota 55439. Copyright © 2015 by Abdo Consulting Group, Inc. International copyrights reserved in all countries. No part of this book may be reproduced in any form without written permission from the publisher. Calico™ is a trademark and logo of Magic Wagon.

Printed in the United States of America, North Mankato, Minnesota.
052014
092014

Written by Jan Fields
Illustrated by Scott Brundage
Edited by Tamara L. Britton, Megan M. Gunderson, and Grace Hansen
Cover and interior design by Candice Keimig

Library of Congress Cataloging-in-Publication Data

Fields, Jan, author.
  Tame Tahoe Tessie / by Jan Fields ; illustrated by Scott Brundage.
     pages cm. -- (Monster hunters)
  Summary: The Discover Cryptids filming crew, also known as the Monster Hunters, head to Lake Tahoe to investigate the monster Tahoe Tessie--but get tangled up in a different kind of mystery instead.
  ISBN 978-1-62402-047-6
1. Monsters--Juvenile fiction. 2. Curiosities and wonders--Juvenile fiction. 3. Video recording--Juvenile fiction. 4. Action photography--Juvenile fiction. 5. Adventure stories. 6. Tahoe, Lake (Calif. and Nev.)--Juvenile fiction. [1. Monsters--Fiction. 2. Curiosities and wonders--Fiction. 3. Video recording--Fiction. 4. Adventure and adventurers--Fiction. 5. Tahoe, Lake (Calif. and Nev.)--Fiction.] I. Brundage, Scott, illustrator. II. Title.
  PZ7.F479177Tam 2015
  813.6--dc23
                              2014005830

TABLE of CONTENTS

chapter 1

A NARROW ESCAPE

Rain dripped from Gabe's thick hair and ran down his nose. With each step, his shoes squished in the mud. As he brushed against cornstalks, they felt like wet fingers sliding across his skin. He peered between the stalks. The Beast of Bray Road could be right on top of them, and they'd never know.

"Have I told you how much I hate being wet?" Sean grumbled.

"No one likes being this wet," said Gabe. He looked around again. "A monster wolf wouldn't want to be out in this rain, would it?"

Gabe missed the baking heat of their last investigation in Texas. Why did he think Wisconsin would be fun? It was probably from

all of Sean's talk about cheese on the trip up there. Since they had arrived in Wisconsin, he hadn't eaten a single slice of cheese. But he'd definitely gotten wet.

Gabe listened for the sound of movement in the cornstalks. All he heard was rain. It was still early evening, but the heavy clouds made it dark. The rain itself made seeing almost impossible. How could they get photos of the beast in pouring rain?

"Come on," Gabe said as he pushed on. He hoped they were nearly at the road. It seemed like they should have been out of the cornfields by now. He ran his hand through his hair, pushing the wet back away from his face. Then he froze. He heard a high, moaning howl coming from behind them!

"Do you think that's the beast?" Gabe whispered.

Sean shrugged, flinging water in Gabe's

direction. "I don't actually believe in the beast."

Then they heard crashing and growling. Something was moving fast through the rows of corn. "That sounds like more than one beast," Sean said, backing away. "And they sound annoyed."

Gabe agreed. He spun and pushed Sean. "Run!" Sean stumbled, but caught himself before he fell. The growls and crashing grew louder. The boys ran faster. Mud and water splattered up to their knees as they pounded along between the corn rows.

Then the toe of Gabe's sneaker caught the edge of a rock. He pitched forward, landing hard in the mud. Sean grabbed Gabe's arm and pulled. "Get up!"

Instead of pulling him to his feet, Sean just dragged Gabe forward nearly a foot. "Let go!" Gabe yelled. "You're not helping."

The animals behind them finally caught up. Gabe heard Sean shriek. Then something big and

four-footed landed on Gabe's back, shoving him face first into the mud.

As Gabe struggled to pull his face out of the mud, he wondered if the Beasts of Bray Road were going to claim their first victims.

When he rolled over, Gabe realized Sean's screams had turned into laughing. Just then, slobber hit Gabe's cheek. Something began licking his face with enthusiasm. Gabe reached up to hold the creature off with one hand, while he wiped at the mud coating his eyes with the other.

Finally, Gabe saw a mud-clotted head that looked like a wolf. If this wasn't the Beast of Bray Road, it sure looked like it. The wolfish-looking animal had tall, pointed ears and a long, toothy muzzle.

Gabe managed to wriggle mostly out from under the beast. "As werewolves go," he said, spitting out mud between words, "they seem very friendly."

"They're not werewolves," Sean said. He pushed his own beast off his chest. "They're malamutes. Really muddy malamutes."

"Is that a kind of wolf?" Gabe asked. The

animal looked a lot like pictures he'd seen of wolves in Wyoming, only with more mud.

"No, they're dogs," Sean said. "They're known for wolfish looks and a friendly disposition toward people. Oh, and size. They're really big."

"I can see that."

Suddenly, an angry man in mud-splattered overalls broke through the corn and into their row. "Bear! Star! Come!" The dogs instantly turned away from Sean and Gabe and dashed over to the man. They stopped directly in front of their master and shook, flinging mud and water everywhere.

"Sit!" the man roared. The dogs sat. Then the man glared at Gabe and Sean. "Now, tell me exactly why you're trespassing on my property."

Gabe held up the waterproof camera. He glanced down at it. It was probably too muddy to take a picture. It was almost too muddy to tell it was a camera. "We're filming for the *Discover*

Cryptids show. It's on the Internet. We had permission to shoot here."

The big man shook his head. "Not on my land you didn't."

"I'm sure we did," Gabe insisted. "My brother Ben is really careful about that kind of thing." Gabe pulled a mud-coated phone from his pocket. "Maybe I should call him."

"That would be a good idea. You may call him from my house. And if I don't like what your brother has to say, the next call will be to the sheriff. Now march!"

Gabe sighed and trudged forward in the direction the man pointed. As he passed, one of the dogs gave him a comforting lick on the hand. At least *they* weren't mad at him. He was pretty sure he wouldn't be able to say the same for Ben when he talked to him.

chapter 2
RIDDLE IN THE LAKE

Two weeks later, the *Discover Cryptids* crew was drier, cleaner, and in a much better mood as they drove up the coast of California as part of a new investigation. They hadn't actually found any answers about the Beast of Bray Road, but they'd met some new people and heard some great stories.

Ben had even patched things up with the farmer who owned the field Gabe and Sean had wandered into. The man understood that his cornfield looked a lot like all the others in the pouring rain. He even gave them all hot chocolate and grilled cheese sandwiches. At least Gabe finally got to eat some cheese in Wisconsin.

Sean pushed an elbow into Gabe's side to get his attention. "Lake Tahoe lies in both California and Nevada. It is the second-deepest lake in the United States," Sean announced, reading from a guidebook. "It holds about 39 trillion gallons of water. If you could dump out all the water in Lake Tahoe, it would fill a container the size and shape of California."

"So how deep is Lake Tahoe?" Gabe asked.

"The average depth is about 1,000 feet," Sean said. "But it reaches 1,645 feet deep in spots."

"That sounds like enough water for a sea monster," Tyler said. "Like the Loch Ness Monster."

Sean groaned. "No, that's a lake monster too. *Loch* means 'lake.'"

"Then what kind of cryptid is a sea monster?" Tyler asked.

"None that I've researched."

"Well what does Tahoe Tessie look like?" Tyler asked.

"According to reports, this creature has a lot in common with the Loch Ness Monster," Sean answered. "It's dark gray or dark blue."

"Any theories about what it is?" Gabe asked.

"That's what we're going to find out this morning," Ben shouted back from the driver's seat. "We're catching a lecture on USOs. I think it'll be a nice contrast with the footage we shot in Nevada from people who claimed to have seen the monster."

"What are USOs?" Tyler asked.

"Unidentified swimming objects," Ben said. "We should hear some rational explanations for Tahoe Tessie at the lecture. I've already gotten permission to film the professor's lecture, so be sure to bring the camera, Gabe."

"Any chance we'll get lunch first?" Tyler asked.

Ben shook his head. "We're barely going to get to the lecture hall on time. We'll eat afterward."

"If I survive," Tyler moaned.

Luckily he did, though not without more complaints and a stop at a snack machine.

Finally they reached the lecture hall and slid into seats near the back. The professor was already standing on the small stage. He was thin with a high forehead and wore jeans and dark-rimmed glasses. A large screen behind him showed a beautiful lake scene with the letters *USO* printed over it. The professor explained that most monster sightings were easily explained, even if people didn't like the explanations.

The professor clicked a button on his remote and the slide changed. It showed a silhouette of a long-necked creature with a small head and a huge back hump. Smaller humps broke the water behind the large one.

"Whenever you're examining something in a lake as big as Lake Tahoe, scale becomes an issue," he explained. "You might be seeing a monster in the distance. Or you might be looking

14

at a mother goose and her goslings." He clicked the button and the slide changed to show a clear photo of the same silhouette, though this time the details of a goose and her goslings were clear.

He showed photo after photo. All the photos looked a lot like sea monsters. Then the professor explained how each was made. "Large fish swimming in groups can look solid when viewed from above," the professor said as he showed a photo of a shadowy creature shot from above the surface of the water. "Thus a fish of 10 feet can become a monster of 30 when swimming with a few of his friends."

The professor clicked his remote again and a large question mark appeared on the screen. "Of course, not every sighting of Tahoe Tessie is easily explained," he said. "I don't claim to have all the answers. I just want to shine a little light in the darkness."

When he finished, the audience applauded

politely. Gabe followed Ben down the aisle to meet the professor.

"Dr. Spencer," Ben said, "I'm Ben Green from *Discover Cryptids*. Your lecture was fascinating. Some of those photos would have fooled me."

The professor smiled. "They fool a lot of people."

"So what do you think about Tahoe Tessie?" Ben asked.

The professor shrugged. "Some sightings are hard to explain. I think it's important to weed out the photos and sightings that are easy to explain. But I've been working with Lake Tahoe conservation for over ten years now, so I've seen some odd things myself."

"I'd like to hear more about what you've seen," Ben said.

The professor stacked up his notes and shoved them into a bag. "Have you been out to the lake yet?"

Ben shook his head.

"Well, I am presently on a project to look at the species in the lake," Dr. Spencer said. "If you guys want to join my crew for a while, I can tell you my stories. And you might get a chance to have your own encounters."

A male voice spoke up from behind Gabe. "Are you sure that's a good idea?"

Gabe turned around and met hostile faces.

A young man about Ben's age crossed his arms. "Don't you remember how the university pulled funding on that archaeology dig because the team claimed to have seen a UFO? How do you think they'll feel about you teaming up with monster hunters?"

"We aren't teaming up. We're helping to uncover truth," the professor said. Then he turned back to Ben. "Allow me to introduce the rest of my team. This is our resident skeptic, David Vincent. And this is Jennifer Lu. They're

my graduate assistants on this project. And this is Jennifer's sister Vicky."

Vicky was a grumpy-looking girl about Gabe's age. Her long black hair was pulled into a ponytail that exactly matched her older sister's.

"Aren't we doing enough babysitting on this project?" David asked.

"Hey!" Jennifer and Vicky snapped in unison, making them look even more alike.

"Let's stay calm," Dr. Spencer said. "Vicky has been a huge help this summer. And I'm sure these guys could be too." He looked toward Gabe and the guys.

"And this is my team," Ben said. "My brother Gabe is our cameraman. And this is Sean and Tyler. They handle research and technical details."

The professor shook hands with each of them, but the graduate students continued to look upset. "Since I'm the boss," Dr. Spencer said, "I'm inviting you again to join us this afternoon."

David muttered something that Gabe didn't catch, but finally Jennifer stepped forward and offered her hand to Ben. "Well, if the professor thinks you'll be a help, that's good enough for me. As he said, he's the boss."

She smiled brightly as she shook hands with each of them. Vicky stood beside David and scowled. She clearly did not want to meet any of them.

"We're heading straight to the lake for an invasive species count," Jennifer said. She turned to look to the professor. "Will these guys be joining us on today's trip?"

The professor nodded. "If they want."

Ben grinned, his eyes focused on Jennifer. "That would be great."

chapter 3
EARLY ANTAGONIST

Jennifer and her sister rode in Ben's van, while the professor and David took the professor's car. Jennifer sat up front next to Ben. Ben kept asking her questions about her work. He said it was interesting and exciting and amazing. Gabe wasn't sure it was *that* great. Then Gabe realized Ben was *flirting* with Jennifer. It was a little gross, actually.

Gabe slumped back against his seat. Beside him, Vicky glared out the window. Gabe sighed. Vicky's head snapped around to look at him so fast he jumped. She stared at him without speaking until he fidgeted uncomfortably.

"So," Gabe said to break the silence. "Do you live near the lake?"

"No," she finally answered. "We live in San Francisco. We're just here for the summer. My sister has *important* work to do."

"So does my brother," Gabe answered.

"Right, *monster* hunting," she said. "That's way more important than *saving the lake*."

He decided to just ignore her rudeness. "Saving the lake from what?"

Vicky rolled her eyes. "Don't you monster hunters do *any* research?"

Sean spoke up from the seat behind them. "Actually, I do extensive research before every investigation. For instance, I know that conservationists are worried about invasive species in Lake Tahoe. The changes caused by invasive species are a problem in waterways all over the United States."

"How?" Tyler asked.

Vicky gave him a look that suggested she thought he was brainless. "They crowd out

native species," she said. "And they cloud the water. Lake Tahoe is so clear and pure. That's one of the most amazing things about it. Invasive species will change that if they're not stopped."

"And Dr. Spencer is trying to get rid of invasive species?" Tyler asked.

"Not exactly. He's counting how many there are and where they live."

"Sounds interesting," Gabe said.

"It's *important*," Vicky said. "Way more important than monster hunting. Jennifer doesn't need the distraction of *monster hunting*." She said this last part loud, leaning forward so her voice would carry to the driver's seat.

Jennifer turned around and gave her sister a fierce look. Then she turned back toward Ben. "Ignore my sister. She usually has much better manners."

This made Vicky's face cloud up even more. She glared out the window again.

"Do you have a place to stay at the lake?" Jennifer asked Ben.

He nodded. "Yes, we booked rooms in one of the lakeside lodges. We were lucky to get rooms at all. Apparently tourism is big this time of year."

Jennifer laughed. "You have no idea. I hope you're ready for some hard work on Dr. Spencer's boat."

Ben turned briefly to grin at her. "We don't mind work. Who knows? Maybe we'll even see Tessie and get some video of her."

Jennifer laughed. "I wouldn't count on that, but you should see interesting fish. And Dr. Spencer can tell you anything you ever wanted to know about the lake. He loves it."

The natural view along the road was beautiful. In every open space, tall pines stood as straight as birthday candles. Gabe could see spots of snow on the mountaintops in the distance.

Jennifer directed Ben toward the dock where

the research boat was tied up. He found one of the last parking spaces, right beside Dr. Spencer's car. Everyone hopped out.

"What are those long poles on the boat?" Tyler asked as he pointed. "The ones that look like they have metal hands on the ends."

"Those are electric probes," Jennifer answered. "Some researchers use big drag nets, but for our fish study, we use these probes. They deliver a mild shock to the fish around the boat that briefly knocks out the fish. They float up, and we can scoop them up in nets."

"Then what?" Gabe asked.

Jennifer laughed. "We count everything. And we tag some of the fish, especially the bass. I will track them to find out how warm-water fish are surviving and breeding in the cold lake."

"What if you shock the water, and Tahoe Tessie floats to the surface?" Tyler asked.

"The mild shocks of the research boat wouldn't knock out something that big," Sean answered. "It would probably just annoy the monster."

Tyler's eyes opened wide. "So we're going out in a little bitty boat to annoy Tahoe Tessie?"

"Tahoe Tessie doesn't exist, you dope," Vicky half shouted. She stomped past all of them to head for the boat. "If it did, I wish it would eat all of you!"

chapter 4

SHOCKING DISCOVERIES

Again Jennifer apologized for her sister. Gabe wondered just how miserable Vicky would make this investigation.

Near the end of the dock, David was messing with the ropes that held the boat to the dock. As they walked toward him, he looked up. "That took you long enough."

"The roads are busy," Ben said mildly.

"We were on the same roads," David said.

"Sorry, I didn't know it was a race," Ben explained.

"Ah, right on time!" Dr. Spencer walked up to them. "We're ready to go."

As they climbed into the boat, Gabe looked across the lake. Many boats were out. Surely

no lake monster would hang around in this crowd. Gabe hoped the fish hunt would be interesting, since it didn't look like they'd get any monster footage.

Dr. Spencer hopped into the boat as David worked quickly to cast off from the dock. Gabe was surprised to see Vicky helping. She moved quickly and seemed to know exactly what to do. Gabe had expected her to sit around like a lump.

As they drove across the lake, Dr. Spencer explained why they needed to head to a shallower part of the lake. "We can't gather fish in the deepest sections of the lake. The water is much too cold there. Fish counts go way up in the shallower, warmer water."

As they rode along, Gabe gazed into the water. "The water is really clear," he said. "But I still can't see the bottom."

"Well, it's a long way down. Probably about 1,000 feet in this spot. Still, we've been losing

water clarity for years," Dr. Spencer explained. "One of the reasons Lake Tahoe is so clear is because of relatively low levels of algae. Algae cloud water, and algae levels are increasing."

"Why?" Ben asked.

"The lake is not naturally very nutrient rich," the researcher explained. "Algae need nutrients to grow. But the introduction of invasive species has changed that. Bottom-feeders stir up the silt. That adds nutrients to the water. Plus, people have dumped a lot of things into the water."

"All kinds of things," Jennifer said, and then laughed. "I've been diving in the lake dozens of times. I've seen signs, pieces of furniture, and stuff I couldn't even guess at."

"We're planning to do some diving," Ben told her. "Some of the reports claim there are underwater caves where Tessie might be hiding. Would you like to come along on a dive?"

"I'd love to. The professor doesn't take the boat out every day."

"I still have to be back at the university every now and then," Dr. Spencer said with a laugh. "In fact, I won't be going out tomorrow. I need to crunch some numbers, so you and David can both be free tomorrow to go diving."

Ben turned toward David with a friendly smile. "Oh, do you dive?"

"I do," the graduate student said. "But I have better things to do on my day off. And you should too, Jennifer. I can't believe we're involved with these guys. Don't you know what this will do to our funding if the university thinks we're using its resources on a monster hunt?"

"I think you should let me worry about that, David," the professor said firmly.

"But you don't seem to be worrying about it at all!"

The professor waved David closer and spoke

to him in a fierce whisper. Gabe could tell David was getting a talk about who was boss of the project.

Ben sighed. "I didn't mean to get your friend in trouble."

"David's a big boy. He'll be fine," Jennifer said. "So we're set for the dive. Are you certified?"

"I am, and so is Gabe," Ben said, and then he turned to offer an apologetic look to the other boys. "I'm afraid you guys will have to sit out that dive."

Tyler looked disappointed, but Sean assured Ben that he would prefer to use the time for more research. "Freezing in the water doesn't sound like fun."

Tyler grumbled about being left out of the good stuff, but his attention was soon drawn away by the busy lake. They saw fishing boats and sailboats and speedboats pulling water skiers.

Finally the boat reached the capture location. Jennifer called Ben over to help swing one probe around to drop into the water off the back of the boat. David and Dr. Spencer swung the other. Each probe opened almost like an umbrella with no cloth over the spines. The tips of the spines would send jolts of electricity into the water.

Sean manned the switch to turn on the electricity. Gabe, Vicky, and Tyler held nets on long poles to scoop up the fish when they surfaced.

"Just try not to drop them in the lake," Vicky said.

Gabe rolled his eyes. He watched the probe drop into the water. Almost immediately, fish began floating slowly up toward the end of the boat.

"The fish won't be stunned long," Jennifer called out. "Scoop them up as soon as they rise enough."

Gabe swung his pole over the end of the boat. He saw fish of all sizes floating upward like a dark cloud. Then he squinted in surprise. He saw something round and gold. It was getting closer. Was it the golden eye of Tahoe Tessie? What if Tyler was right and they'd jolted the water just enough to annoy the lake monster?

chapter 5

MAN
OVERBOARD

"We've got another goldfish," Jennifer shouted.

"That thing's huge!" Tyler said as Vicky scooped it up.

"It's about five pounds," Jennifer said, picking the fish out of the net. "We've scooped a few that were larger. This is our newest problem fish. Goldfish muck up the water with their bottom-feeding habits."

"How do goldfish get into the lake?" Gabe asked.

"Probably from people dumping aquariums into the lake," Dr. Spencer said. "They think it's okay. Goldfish are little. But they don't stay little when they're in a big lake full of food."

They continued to scoop fish from the lake. They collected several largemouth bass and some bluegills. Jennifer hauled one of the big bass over and flopped it onto a table. "A bass will eat anything that fits in its mouth." She used a finger to open the fish's huge mouth. "As you can see, a lot of our native fish could fit in there. That's why I decided to do my thesis on warm-water fish like this. We need to know how they're surviving and breeding here."

Sean walked over to look at the gasping fish. "What will you do with him?"

"It's a her. I'll tag her. Then we can find out where she goes in winter when this shallower water freezes solid."

They spent the rest of the day on the boat. The guys helped with tagging the fish. Tyler complained about it being disgusting since it involved cutting into the fish to plant the tag.

They moved frequently to new spots in the water. Over and over, they swung the nets around and hauled out loads of fish.

Finally, Dr. Spencer called for a break. "I'll drive out to a deeper spot and we'll eat."

"Great!" Tyler said. "I didn't want to mention how close I was to starvation."

The boat moved along the lake at a good clip, though it definitely wasn't a speedboat. With the long probe poles rising into the air on either side of the boat, it looked a bit like some kind of water bug. They moved to a quieter part of the lake and stopped, letting the boat drift gently as they ate.

"You won't see as many boats over here," Dr. Spencer said. "The water is 1,600 feet deep. The fishing isn't as good, and it's too cold for water-skiing."

"It's still an interesting spot," Jennifer said. She pointed off into the distance. "I read an old newspaper account from the *San Francisco Chronicle* when I was a kid. It was about two hikers who said they spotted Tahoe Tessie swimming in the water over there."

Vicky frowned at her sister. "I didn't know that you ever paid attention to that silly monster story."

"I was curious. I wanted to know what sort of animal might be confused with a monster."

"Do you have any theories?" Ben asked.

Jennifer shrugged. "Well, you heard some of the professor's theories in his USO lecture. I also think there's a chance that it might have been a trout. The lake form of Lahontan cutthroat trout grow to be over 40 pounds. They are native to

Lake Tahoe, so they've been in the lake for all the years covered in these monster stories. And they're rare enough for sightings to confuse people."

"But 40 pounds isn't nearly big enough for some of the reports," Sean said.

Jennifer shrugged. "Several big trout in a school might be confused with one large animal swimming. The newspaper story I mentioned described a 17-foot swimming creature. It wouldn't take too many trout to create that kind of illusion."

"Sounds like a solid theory," Ben said.

Gabe looked out across the lake while he ate his sandwich. Then he jolted to attention, squinting against the sun. He was certain he'd seen something break the surface closer to the far shore. "Did anyone see that?"

"See what?" Ben asked, immediately turning to look toward the shore.

"A figment of Gabe's imagination," Vicky suggested.

Gabe ignored her. "I'm not sure. Something broke the surface over there. It looked pretty big."

"Could it have been one of those big fish?" Tyler asked.

Gabe shrugged. "I don't know. I just saw something."

"It's a lake," Vicky said dryly. "It's full of somethings."

Gabe sighed. "Yeah, it just surprised me." He crossed to the back of the boat, where David was messing with the probes. Gabe leaned out as far as he dared. He scanned the water, but he didn't see anything.

He began to straighten up again. Just then, one of the probes swung hard and smacked Gabe in the back. Gabe was too close to the back of the boat to catch his balance. He flew over the side and into the ice-cold water.

chapter 6

UNDERWATER ENCOUNTER

The water sent a shock of icy cold through Gabe's body. His sodden clothes and shoes slowed his strokes. Finally he made it to the surface.

"Gabe!" Ben yelled. "Grab the net."

Gabe felt as if he were moving in slow motion. He reached out and caught the metal rim of the net, but his stiff fingers just slid off.

"Shove your arm into the net," Dr. Spencer yelled.

Gabe shoved his arm down deep into the net until the rim rested under his armpit. Then he flung the other arm in too. Ben hauled the net and Gabe to the side of the boat. Hands reached out and dragged him aboard.

"You need to be more careful," Dr. Spencer said as he wrapped a blanket around Gabe. His teeth chattered so hard he couldn't talk.

"It's my fault," David said. "I didn't know the kid was messing around at the end of the boat. I was working on that stiff swing arm on the probe and managed to bump him."

If Gabe's teeth stopped chattering, he'd tell them it was a lot more than a bump.

"Well, that's it for today," Dr. Spencer said. "We'll head back so Gabe can change and warm up. We can get back on the water the day after tomorrow. Your team is still welcome along, Ben."

"Really?" David said. "After they cost us half a day? Shouldn't we leave the day care on the shore? Maybe the monster hunters could babysit Vicky, too."

"Now that's just uncalled for," Jennifer said.

"What do you think the university is going to

say about this?" David said. "Like the monster hunting isn't unprofessional enough. We're also dragging little kids along on a serious research expedition where they can get hurt."

"Hey," Tyler said. "You're the guy who knocked him into the water."

"Ben's team was a big help today," the professor said. "In fact, we probably got as much done this morning as we would normally do all day since we had so many extra hands. So they're welcome to come back out with us."

"I appreciate that," Ben said. "I'll let you know."

The rest of the ride back to the dock was fairly quiet. Vicky had extended her glares to include David, though he barely noticed. Gabe's teeth finally stopped chattering, but he didn't feel much like talking. His shoulders ached from hauling the nets all morning, and his back hurt from being smacked by the probe.

When they finally returned to the dock, Gabe expected his brother to ask how he was doing. But Ben seemed to have forgotten Gabe's accident as soon as Gabe stopped shivering. Instead, he offered Jennifer a ride to wherever she was staying. As they walked together up the dock, Gabe half expected them to hold hands. He found it all very embarrassing. His brother was usually so cool.

Vicky stomped along beside him, glaring at anyone who got in her line of sight. Gabe kept telling himself that she was just a girl. He should ignore her. Still, it was hard to ignore that laser-beam glare.

When they caught up to Ben at the van, he turned cheerfully to them. "I'm half tempted to cancel our lodge rooms and just camp with Vicky and Jennifer."

Vicky made a gagging noise. "I would prefer to stay in an actual room with Wi-Fi," Sean said.

"Research is a part of this investigation too. And I want to read about the giant goldfish. And I want to sleep in an actual bed."

"Camping is fun," Tyler insisted.

Sean looked at Tyler as if he were crazy. "Mosquitoes, wildlife, and snakes. What is fun about that?"

Jennifer smiled at the squabbling boys. "I'm afraid it would be hard to get a site at the campground anyway. It's really packed."

"Well, we'll stick with the lodge then," Ben said. "We'll see you bright and early tomorrow for the dive."

"I'm looking forward to it," Jennifer said. Something about her tone of voice drew another gagging sound from her sister. Gabe had to admit, it made him feel a little nauseated too.

Even after the long day, Gabe was glad they'd be diving tomorrow. He didn't get to dive much. None of the investigations he'd been on so far

for *Discover Cryptids* had taken them anywhere near deep water.

The next morning dawned bright and unusually warm for the area. Gabe doubted it would do much to warm the icy water. He was glad for his thick wet suit. Tyler helped them check the equipment. "I wish I were going with you."

"You can come on the boat if you want," Ben said. "It's never a bad idea to have someone stay topside to keep an eye on things."

"And watch you have all the fun," Tyler grumbled.

"You can bring snacks," Ben suggested.

Tyler perked up. "Well in that case!"

Sean passed on the invitation. He was editing footage they'd shot during the fish netting. Tyler helped haul the camera and diving equipment.

Jennifer had rented a small fishing boat for the day. It had a tiny cabin and seats all around

the deck. As they headed out into deep water, Jennifer and Ben stood shoulder to shoulder at the controls. In loud voices, they sang the theme song to *Gilligan's Island*, a television show from before anyone on the boat was born.

Finally they anchored at a diving spot not far from where Gabe had fallen in the day before. Jennifer raised a red-and-white striped diving flag. Then the four divers did a final equipment check and pulled on flippers and tanks. Jennifer and Vicky sat on the back of the boat and rolled over backwards into the water. When they were clear, Ben and Gabe did the same.

As always, Gabe felt the initial shock of transitioning from topside to under the water. Everything felt different. You saw things differently. You moved differently. Even sounds were weird and alien. And it was *much* warmer in the wet suit than in his wet clothes the day before.

The water was very clear. It reminded Gabe of diving in the Gulf of Mexico. Of course, in Lake Tahoe, he wasn't going to see any dolphins. In fact, Jennifer had warned them that they might not see any fish at all.

The four of them gathered in a group under the water. Jennifer made hand gestures to show them where they were going. Then she began the slow swim down. Vicky and Gabe followed closely behind her. Ben took up the rear.

The diving weights on his belt helped fight Gabe's natural tendency to float. His legs and the flexible fins on his feet did most of the work of moving him through the water.

As they swam deeper, the water grew murkier. Gabe kept a sharp eye on Jennifer up ahead and Vicky off to his right. Tiny specks of debris floated in the water around him.

At last they reached the bottom of the lake. They swam leisurely along the bottom. Gabe

realized that if the lake did hold a monster, it would have no trouble sneaking up on them down there. Even the other divers looked a little blurry through the silty water. It was almost like following ghosts.

Jennifer signaled that something was just ahead. Then she sped up, swimming fast enough to turn into a fuzzy blob in Gabe's vision. He swam after her, and then froze at the sight just ahead.

He could only see Jennifer from the waist down. Her head and shoulders had disappeared into the mouth of a giant fish! Her legs moved sluggishly. For a moment, Gabe felt a jolt of panic. Tahoe Tessie was real, and much more dangerous than anyone knew!

He swam faster, hurrying to help. Ben swam by him but didn't seem to be in any hurry to save Jennifer. Instead his brother held up a camera and took photos. Gabe looked between Jennifer

and Ben. His brother certainly wouldn't let a monster fish eat his potential new girlfriend. Vicky flashed by him in the water and took up a spot sitting on the giant fish's head.

Gabe realized it was made from stone, or maybe cement. He rubbed his hand over the algae-covered surface. Jennifer swam out of the fish's mouth. Ben tapped Gabe's arm and pointed at the camera. Of course, Gabe was supposed to be filming for the show.

Feeling sheepish about forgetting, Gabe shot footage of the big cement fish as the other divers swam around it. Ben stuck his head into the fish. He looked like the undersea version of a lion tamer.

The more they climbed on the fish or touched it, the more silt and algae floated up into the water. Visibility grew even worse. Gabe wondered if divers had ever mistaken the big stone fish for Tahoe Tessie.

This was the area where Tahoe Tessie was spotted most often. He knew some of the reports spoke of underwater caves. Could there be any nearby? He really couldn't see anything in the murky water.

Suddenly, Gabe spotted movement at the very outer reaches of visibility. Had one of the divers left the rest of the group? He turned back, counting the number of shadowy figures swimming around the fish. All three were there.

He turned away from them again, straining to make out anything in the swirling silt. He swam toward the gray gloom. Then he saw movement again.

Gabe filmed into the gloom, moving farther and farther from the group. What was he seeing? Could it be Tahoe Tessie? The current now swirled silt all around him from his movements. Suddenly, he felt something grab his ankle. It felt like someone's hand.

He jerked his foot, but he couldn't get free. The grip tightened. Kicking and pulling clouded the water so much Gabe couldn't even see his foot. He was stuck. If he could get his brother's attention, he knew Ben could get him free. But as he turned, he realized he'd drifted farther from the group than he'd thought. He could no longer see them. As far as Gabe could tell, he was trapped alone at the bottom of Lake Tahoe with the lake monster.

chapter 7

A CLOSE CALL

The number one diving rule is never, ever dive alone. Swimming away from the rest of the group was about the same as diving alone. Gabe jerked his leg again and again, but he couldn't get free.

Gabe told himself to calm down. Panic would only make him use up oxygen. He remembered his diving instructor talking about the danger of panic while diving. Gabe stopped thrashing. He concentrated on breathing normally. Then he turned on the camera light.

He slowly bent over and shone the camera light directly at his ankle. Loops of thick rope were wound tightly around his ankle. The ends disappeared into a nearby pile of broken rock.

Slowly and carefully, he tugged at the loops until one was loose enough to slip over his flipper. That added enough slack to the remaining loops to slip free.

Gabe looked around again. He knew he couldn't be that far from the group. All he had to do was swim straight back until he ran into the giant cement fish. Of course, he'd gotten turned around while struggling with the rope. Plus, the currents had pushed him.

Still, he could swim to the surface and find

the boat easily enough–right? Gabe wasn't ready to give up. He moved forward slowly, sweeping the camera light back and forth. As he swam, he wondered about the moving shadow he'd seen. Had he caught a glimpse of Tahoe Tessie?

Suddenly, the swirling water ahead of him grew agitated. A diver burst through the gloom. Gabe recognized Ben immediately. From his brother's sharp gestures, Gabe guessed that Ben was mad.

Gabe held up a hand and nodded. Then he pointed behind him. He pointed to his eyes through the swim mask. He gestured with his hands to show he'd seen something big. Ben stopped waving his hands around and peered past Gabe. Gabe turned to look in the same direction. Nothing appeared in the gloom.

When he turned back around, Gabe saw Jennifer and Vicky appear on either side of Ben. Ben didn't pay attention to them. Instead, he tapped the camera and made Gabe's gesture for "something big." Gabe nodded. He had filmed the thing he saw.

Ben turned to Jennifer and gestured up. Jennifer nodded. She waved for them to follow her. They swam along the bottom through the murky water. Gabe followed closely. He didn't want to get into any more trouble.

They swam past the big concrete fish. Finally they were back to the point where they'd begun their dive. They slowly swam to the surface, pausing at different points to wait for their bodies to get used to the change in pressure. Gabe knew that swimming to the surface too fast made air bubbles in your body. Those bubbles hurt. They might even kill you. Ben and Gabe's diving coach had gone over that point several times.

Finally, they broke the surface close to the boat. As soon as they all gathered in a small

circle, Ben pulled the air regulator out of his mouth and said, "Don't ever scare me like that again."

"I won't," Gabe said. "I'm sorry. I didn't realize I'd drifted so much when I saw the thing in the water."

"You filmed it?"

Gabe nodded. "But the water is so cloudy. I don't know if I got it. And I had another problem."

"A problem?" Ben echoed.

Before Gabe could explain about his ankle, they heard a yell from the boat. Tyler was standing up, waving his arms at them. They turned and swam toward the boat.

When they reached the boat, Tyler yelled, "Did you guys see that?"

"See what?" Ben asked.

"The thing in the water! I think I saw Tahoe Tessie!"

chapter 8
A FLEETING GLIMPSE

Ben, Jennifer, and Gabe scanned the water around them. "When did you see it?" Ben asked.

"Just before you guys popped up," Tyler said. "Something passed under the boat a couple of times."

"You guys are so fake," Vicky half shouted. "There's no monster in this lake." She swam to the boat and pulled herself out of the water.

Tyler made a face at her, but reached out to help haul her into the boat. "I didn't say it was a monster. But I saw something, and it didn't swim like a fish."

Gabe grabbed the side of the boat and hauled himself out. Tyler reached out to help. He noticed Vicky didn't offer to lend a hand. Instead she sat

back with her arms crossed. Gabe ignored her and scanned the water around the boat.

Finally Ben and Jennifer climbed aboard. As soon as they had settled in, Vicky scrambled over to get up in Ben's face. "Don't use my sister in your monster hunting scam! You'll wreck this whole project."

"I'm not going to do anything to hurt your sister," Ben insisted.

"Right. Sure." Vicky slumped back into one of the boat chairs and crossed her arms again.

The rest of the group stared into the water for several minutes. No one caught sight of anything. "I saw something before," Tyler insisted. "I did."

Ben clapped him on the shoulder. "I believe you. Gabe saw something under the water. When we get back and see what he shot, maybe we'll get some answers." Then he turned back to Gabe. "You said you had another problem under there?"

Gabe reluctantly told them about getting tangled in the rope.

"That's it! No more wandering off on a dive. What if you didn't get loose? What if we didn't find you? You could have run out of air." With each sentence, Ben's voice got a little louder.

"I know," Gabe said. "I won't do anything like that again."

Ben finally calmed down and started up the motor. Jennifer directed them closer to the land. "There are underwater caves," she said. "Though I've not had a chance to see them. We've been so busy with the research. Since we didn't have time to check them out today, you guys might want to come back tomorrow."

"But Dr. Spencer invited us to join him," Tyler said.

"I'm sure it's more important to do what you actually came to Lake Tahoe for," Jennifer said.

"I'm sure there will be time for both," Ben

said. "I know I would love to spend the day out with you. Um, I mean out on the research project."

Gabe crossed to the other side of the boat to avoid the mushy conversation. To his surprise, Vicky followed him. "Could you talk your brother out of following us around?"

Gabe looked at her in surprise. "I guess that's up to your sister. If she doesn't want us around, she can just say so."

"I don't know." Vicky flopped down on the seat beside Gabe. "She's acting goofy. She's usually all about the work. I'm surprised she doesn't agree with David about the monster hunting."

"We're not just monster hunting. We want to know the truth about what people are seeing in the water," Gabe said. "I saw something. So did Tyler. We're not making it up."

"Sure."

Gabe gave up on the crabby girl. He got up
and sat near Tyler. They compared what they'd
seen, though neither had much detail. Whatever
Tyler saw had stayed deep enough to be a blur.

Back at the dock, they had to wait through
another mushy goodbye scene between Ben
and Jennifer. Then they drove back to the
lodge. Gabe was eager to see what his camera
had recorded.

In the room, Sean plugged the camera into the laptop. The footage of the giant cement fish was great. Everyone laughed when Ben stuck his head in the fish's mouth.

"Where would something like that come from?" Tyler asked.

"My guess is that it came from a mini-golf course. At one time, I expect people hit their golf balls into the fish's mouth and they came out at the back."

Tyler laughed. "A fish that poops golf balls! How did it end up in the lake?"

Ben shrugged. "That I don't know. People have a tendency to use lakes, rivers, and the ocean as one big garbage dump."

When they got to Gabe's footage of the swirling water, the images were far less clear. They saw what might have been something moving in the water. Or it might have been a thick pocket of silt moving in the current.

"I'm afraid there's nothing there that can't be explained by a natural event," Ben said. "It will still make great footage for the show. I want to show how Lake Tahoe has many natural things that can look like monsters."

"It looked more like something alive when I looked at it directly," Gabe said, but then he wondered if it really did. Maybe he just wanted to *think* he saw the monster. After all, he'd been pretty sure some person grabbed his leg, but it had turned out to just be rope.

Ben looked closely at the screen when they reached the footage where Gabe had used the camera like a flashlight. It clearly showed the rope around Gabe's ankle and the way it was wedged in the rock. "That's weird," Ben said.

"It was scary," Gabe said.

Ben nodded. He froze the image and stared for another moment. "It doesn't really look natural. The rope looks like it was wedged in the rock."

"It could have been caught in the current," Sean said, "and dragged into the crack in the rock."

"I suppose." Ben didn't sound convinced, but he unfroze the image and they watched the rest of the footage. Then he announced it was time to go out and eat.

"Are we going out with Dr. Spencer tomorrow?" Gabe asked.

"I'll give him a call and find out." Ben pulled out his phone and stepped away to make the call.

"I can't wait for another day of watching Ben swoon over some girl," Tyler said.

"And hang out with crabby Vicky," Gabe added.

"Actually I think Vicky is interesting," Sean said. "I wouldn't mind discussing some of my research with her."

"Yeah, have fun with that," Tyler said.

Ben walked back over to the group. He looked really down. "Well, we won't be going out with the professor tomorrow. The university heard about Gabe's accident on the research boat. They ordered all minors off the boat. The professor said he's going to try to get the ban lifted, but for tomorrow we'll be on our own."

"So what will we do?" Gabe asked.

"We can rent a boat and go back out to that area where we were diving," Ben said. "Oh, Vicky is coming with us. She's a minor too, so she can't go out with the professor until he gets the ban lifted. It'll be great."

"Oh yeah," Gabe said as Tyler groaned. "It'll be terrific."

chapter 9

An Elusive Beast

The next day, Gabe could barely drag himself out of bed. He felt like a long, yawning day of misery stretched out in front of him. Without Jennifer along, Vicky was sure to be even more crabby.

Gabe and Tyler moped over their cereal, while Ben wolfed down a piece of toast.

"If Vicky insults me all day, I'm not making any promises about my behavior," Tyler announced.

"I expect you guys to be nice," Ben replied. "We have a job to do, and Vicky can be a big help. You saw how much she helps Dr. Spencer."

"Yeah," Tyler said. "But she likes him. She hates us."

Gabe looked up at his brother and shook his head. Did Ben really think Vicky would lift one hand to help them? Just then, they heard a knock at the door. It was Jennifer and Vicky.

"I hope I'm not too early," Jennifer said. "Dr. Spencer likes to get an early start."

"You're fine," Ben said. "We'll be sure to show Vicky a good time. She can help us shoot some video around that diving area from yesterday."

"What a great idea," Jennifer said, patting her sister's rigid shoulder. "Well, I need to go."

As soon as Jennifer left, Vicky turned to them with a big toothy smile. "I know the perfect place to shoot today!"

Ben raised an eyebrow. "Oh?"

"I heard something cool last night," Vicky said. "Someone told me of the exact spot where a bunch of people have seen Tahoe Tessie recently. I can show you guys how to get there. It's not far from where we were yesterday."

"I thought you didn't believe in Tahoe Tessie," Tyler said, crossing his arms.

She shrugged. "I don't. But a scientist needs an open mind."

"That's true," Sean agreed.

Gabe glared at his friend. Whose side was Sean on? As they gathered up cameras and headed outside, Gabe worried about exactly what Vicky had in mind.

They were able to rent the exact same boat again. Ben declared it was a good sign for the day. Vicky offered to drive.

"You can navigate," Ben said firmly. "I drive."

Vicky gave in and sat near Sean. He immediately launched into some boring talk about methods of navigation. Vicky just stared at him, but Sean didn't seem to notice. He never did when he was in full fact-spouting mode.

They crossed the lake, carefully following all the markers and watching for other boats. The

ride took long enough for Gabe to wish he'd brought a hat to keep the sun off his head.

"We should have packed lunch," Tyler complained.

"We'll be there soon," Vicky said. "We can tie up on the way back and get some hot dogs from a stand I know about. It's not that far."

"Great," Ben said. He smiled at Tyler. "See, I told you that Vicky would be lots of help."

"I'll believe it when I taste the hot dog," Tyler said.

After a few minutes, Vicky spoke up again. "The spot we're going isn't far now."

Ben turned and drove the boat parallel to the lakeshore for a while. Then they entered a narrow branch off the lake.

Banks rose up steeply. The tall pines blocked some of the sun. Gabe felt a chill breeze sweep across the lake. "Wow, that's a big drop in temperature."

"Good thing we're not planning on swimming," Tyler added.

"That's why you don't see as many boats over here," Vicky said. "It's pretty deep and the water is very cold. There aren't many game fish, and no one wants to water-ski around here."

"But the monster comes here?" Gabe asked.

"That's what I heard," Vicky said, smiling brightly again.

Gabe didn't find her smile comforting at all.

They came around a sharp bend in the inlet. Just ahead, something huge and dark rose out of the water. A series of humps broke the water in a row. "Monster!" Tyler yelled, scrambling for the camera on the seat beside him.

Gabe half stood, pulling the video camera up to shoot. His heart pounded in his chest. Were they going to get proof right there? That's when something odd finally broke through Gabe's

excitement. The "monster" wasn't moving, not even a little.

Ben brought the boat close to the tall "head" of the figure. They all saw it was a boulder standing tall in the water. Several smaller boulders formed the other humps. As they stared up at the rock formation, Vicky's howling laughter rang out behind them.

"I guess I proved one thing," she said between giggles. "You guys will believe *anything!*"

"That's not funny," Tyler yelled. He stormed over to the laughing girl and gave her a shove.

She shoved him back and snapped, "What's the matter, can't monster hunters take a joke?"

Gabe looked at the rock formation with interest. Sure, it was a rotten joke, but it did look a lot like a monster. "Ben," he called. "This might be the source of some reports. Should I shoot here?"

"Yeah." Ben turned to smile at Vicky. "You

might have shown us something useful after all. And Tyler, don't push guests."

"Okay, I got it," Gabe said. "Should we shoot some other angles? Maybe away from the rocks?"

"Good idea," Ben said.

"Are you planning to put some fake video up to fool people?" Vicky asked. "I knew that was the kind of show you did!"

"That's not the kind of show we do," Gabe said. "But these rocks could be the source of some of the sightings. Ben will show them as one explanation."

"Sure he will," Vicky said.

"You know, it's about time you let up," Gabe said. "Our show isn't what you think. Did you even watch it?"

"As if I would watch something like that," Vicky said.

"You guys should sit down," Ben warned. "No roughhousing in the boat."

Gabe turned back to filming, but Tyler stood up again and shouted at Vicky, "You don't know anything about us!"

"I know fakers when I see them," she said.

Then Sean's voice interrupted everything. "What's that?"

Gabe and Tyler turned to see Sean pointing into the water. A dark shadow swam toward the boat. It passed under them and something banged against the underside of the boat. Gabe, Tyler, and Vicky all jumped in surprise, knocking themselves off balance. They windmilled their arms, trying to catch their balance. Tyler managed to throw himself at the boat's deck. Gabe and Vicky weren't as lucky. They tumbled into the water.

The ice-cold water slammed into Gabe just as it had two days ago. His life jacket helped him reach the surface almost instantly.

Tyler and Sean reached over the side to grab his arms and haul him in.

"Gabe!" Ben yelled. "Where is Vicky?"

"There!" Sean yelled, pointing nearby. "She's still under."

Gabe looked in the direction Sean pointed. He let go of Sean's arm, but kept a grip on Tyler's hand. Then he turned to reach out with his free hand. "I'll get her."

He could see Vicky clearly. She was flailing wildly just under the surface. Her life jacket kept her from sinking deeply, but she seemed to be fighting the water while gripping her leg. Gabe reached for her one free arm, only to be smacked by her flailing.

Suddenly something dark rose out of the water. For an instant, Gabe thought of Tahoe Tessie, but then he realized he was looking at a diver in full gear. The person caught Vicky around the waist and hauled her to the surface.

Vicky coughed out water as soon as she

broke the surface. Gabe climbed into the boat as the diver towed Vicky over. Tyler, Sean, and Ben hauled them out of the water.

Gabe flopped onto the deck of the boat, shivering. He made up his mind to stay out of Lake Tahoe for the rest of the trip.

"Jennifer?" Gabe turned sharply at Ben's voice. His brother was staring at the diver in confusion. "What are you doing here?"

"I'll explain," Jennifer said. "But can we warm up my sister first?"

"Yes, please," Vicky said through chattering teeth.

Luckily the boat had two thick oilskins. Gabe and Vicky were quickly wrapped up like burritos. Vicky rubbed her right calf. "I got a cramp," she gasped out. "I couldn't swim."

"Extremely cold water frequently causes severe cramps," Sean said calmly. "You could have drowned."

Vicky nodded. Her sister put an arm around her. "I guess I owe you an explanation."

"You're the one who banged something against the bottom of the boat," Ben said.

She nodded. "I never expected anyone to end up in the water. David talked me into it. He's the one who knocked Gabe into the water that first day. Then he wrapped the rope around Gabe's leg when you were diving. He figured if you got scared enough for your brother's safety, you'd leave."

Ben looked hurt. "You want us to leave too?"

"I'm sorry. I just don't want to risk this project. Without it, I can't finish my thesis. I can't complete my degree." She paused, and added reluctantly, "And David and I wouldn't be able to take a lucrative job we were offered with a game fishing company. It's all dependent on our findings about the bass."

"So this was about money?" Gabe asked.

She looked at him, ashamed. "I guess."

"So is David out there swimming around the boat too?" Ben asked.

She shook her head. "He was taking too many risks, especially with the rope thing yesterday. I was afraid someone was going to get hurt. So I told Vicky to bring you out here. I planned to bang on the boat a few times and tangle a chain in your propeller if you stopped. I figured being stuck on the lake for a few hours would kill your enthusiasm for the hunt." She sighed again. "And then I planned a big noisy fight with you tonight. I figured that would be enough to get you to leave since you seemed to like me."

Ben crossed his arms. "Well, you don't have to worry about that part anymore. Do we need to untangle the propeller?"

She shook her head. "I didn't get to that part. You have to believe me. I never intended to hurt anyone."

Ben nodded. "I certainly believe you never intended to hurt your sister. Let's get these guys back so they can warm up." He turned back to the controls.

"There's something in the water!" Tyler yelled. "And this time it's really big."

They all raced to the sides of the boat. Even Gabe and Vicky flung off their oilskins to join the others. Gabe grabbed a camera. He pointed it at the water as a huge shadow passed beneath the boat. This one was longer than the entire length of the boat.

"What was that?" Tyler asked.

"A school of trout," Jennifer suggested, though she didn't sound very sure.

Then Gabe tilted the camera up in the direction the shadow had gone. Closer to the shore, he saw something rise up out of the water. "Look!"

Everyone turned. The hump was as high as

a boulder and two darker, shining humps broke the surface behind it. Then they disappeared into the lake.

"It's real," Jennifer whispered.

"And we have it on video!" Gabe said. Ben and the guys gathered around him, thumping him on the back in celebration.

"I guess this proves one thing," Tyler said. "Nothing keeps the monster hunters down. Not even girls!"

The guys all laughed as Jennifer and Vicky struck matching poses, arms crossed and glaring.